A Magical Christmas

Dr. Adyasha Acharya

Ukiyoto Publishing

All global publishing rights are held by

Ukiyoto Publishing

Published in 2024

Content Copyright © Dr. Adyasha Acharya

ISBN 9789361720161
*All rights reserved.
No part of this publication may be reproduced,
transmitted, or stored in a retrieval system, in any form
by any means, electronic, mechanical, photocopying,
recording or otherwise, without the prior permission of
the publisher.*

The moral rights of the authors have been asserted.

*This is a work of fiction. Names, characters, businesses,
places, events, locales, and incidents are either the
products of the author's imagination or used in a fictitious
manner. Any resemblance to actual persons, living or
dead, or actual events is purely coincidental.*

*This book is sold subject to the condition that it shall not by
way of trade or otherwise, be lent, resold, hired out or
otherwise circulated, without the publisher's prior
consent, in any form of binding or cover other than that in
which it is published.*

www.ukiyoto.com

Dedicated to my family, friends and readers.

Avia

Christmas is my favourite time of the year. There are celebrations, presents, decorations, colourful lights. There is no one who does not like Christmas time.

"Avia," my father calls from the garage. "I have bought the tree decorations."

"Be there in a sec, Dad."

I hurry outside to help Dad bring the cartons inside. Mom is busy baking cookies with my grandmother.

Our house is always lively and chaotic during Christmas holidays. The good kind of chaotic, I mean.

I work here in the Icehaven Town as a writer. My family is full of nerds. Dad and Mom are the chief editors in the Icehaven Daily Newsletter and I manage the fiction and cover stories department.

"Put those near the tree, you two," Mom orders from the kitchen.

"Yes, Mrs. Heming," Dad salutes at her.

Mom rolls her eyes then gets back to her baking. I take mostly from Dad, his blonde hair and blue eyes rather than Mom's brunette curls and onyx irises.

"Dad, I have to go and the buy the candies and champagne for the Christmas party tomorrow night," I tell Dad as we set the boxes besides the tree in the corner.

Every year, us, the Hemings hold a grand Christmas celebration party in our town and invite all the townsfolk. We have already handed out the invitations for tomorrow and almost everything has been set.

The only things left are champagne, candies, flowers and confirmation from the caterer. And the photographer too. Since my best friend, Claire's family is catering; I don't have to worry about that part at all. It is all set.

I grab my keys from the shelf and my pink leather jacket. Even though I am wearing my sweater, I need the jacket, gloves, winter cap and my boots. Icehaven is particularly known for its chilly winters. Hence, the name.

The road has been covered with a thin layer of snow. I am glad my Ford has good tyres. Dad uses a truck so the snow doesn't bother him much.

I reach my stop in ten minutes. After buying a full box of some French wine, I head to the candy and snacks shop. I just hope I don't finish the candies myself that I shall buy for the kids for the party tomorrow night.

Just as I am about to open the door, it is pulled inside and I crash into someone.

"Oh, I'm really sorry," I quickly apologize not caring to figure out whose mistake it was exactly. It is Christmas time, who bothers with all this.

"No, it is my fault," a familiarly attractive voice responds.

"Enin," the name leaves my lips before I can comprehend.

"Hey, Avia. How have you been?"

Enin and I dated for two years before he left without telling me. His dad passed away suddenly from a car accident. The road was slippery and his car skid. It was horrific. Enin was away on a photography tour in Europe.

He returned just after his dad breathed his last. He can't stop blaming and torturing himself for that moment ever since.

He cut himself off from the whole world only focusing in his job. His mother too left few months after to stay with her sister. Enin's aunt too lives in New York where he was currently working in a company as a chief photographer.

The smile and cocky grin has permanently disappeared from his face. I don't remember Enin ever being sad before his dad's death. Whenever I had a bad day, he would cheer me up.

He was such a lively and active guy. Now he is carrying the burden of his dad's death and I am sure he is not going to get it off anytime soon.

I finally find my voice to speak up. "I wasn't expecting to see you here."

"I wasn't expecting to be here too. But Mom wanted to celebrate Christmas at our house this time and I couldn't deny her obviously."

I nod solemnly. Honestly, these two years have been difficult without him. And I am really happy to see him. But the hurt still lingers like shadow over my face.

He left me and never made an attempt to contact me in these past two years. I texted him once asking him how he was to which he just replied he is coping.

I didn't text him after that and he didn't make efforts too.

"Before you say anything else," Enin says quickly. "I think we should talk."

I stare at him confused. "There is nothing to talk, Enin. You did what you thought was right back then."

"I was disturbed. I wasn't even thinking straight."

"Yeah, but we had months after that. You never reached out. Not even once." I feel bad for shouting at him but I wasn't expecting to see him ever at all.

Yet, here he is standing in front of me, all green eyes and raven hair. That handsome face I had missed for so long.

"Look, I know it was hard for you. I would have waited for you had you just said you wanted me to. But you didn't. We could have done it together, Enin. I didn't even want to leave you. But you left me with no other choice." Tears pool in my eyes.

This is so not the time and place to have this conversation at all. I have plans for tomorrow and work to do.

And as much as it hurts to see the man I fell in love with in front of me, I can't let my past ruin my time with my family.

"I can't do this right now. And I don't want to hurt you or myself anymore. You made your decision and I have to learn to live with it." I wipe my eyes with my handkerchief. "Merry Christmas, Enin. Give your regards to your mom."

......

Enin

Avia turns on her heels and goes into the shop leaving me standing there like a goddamn statue.

I knew I had screwed up. Bad. And I don't even know how to fix this anymore. I made a wrong choice. I should have hung onto our love instead of pushing her away.

I thought I was doing a favour by letting her go since I wasn't oriented at that time. Dad's death had turned me into a shell. And I didn't Avia to be attached to an emotionless guy.

Guess I was too stupid.

Now I have lost the two most important people in my life. One, I can never bring back and the second one will never come back to me after what I did to her.

I literally deserve an award for the most foolish guy ever.

Hurrying across the street, I disappear before Avia comes out of the shop. I don't want to torture her anymore. I start the engine and drive back home.

Mom is busy reading the newspaper when I return. "Avia writes such beautiful stories," she keeps mumbling to herself when I return.

She doesn't just write beautiful stories; she is one herself. And I lost this story from my book.

"Honey," she places the book onto the tea table in front of her and looks up at me. "What happened?" she must have read my face.

"I ran into her," I say flopping down on the couch. Covering my face with my hands, I close my eyes. This couldn't be the way it is ending.

"What did she say?"

"Yeah, well she hates me. She doesn't even hate waiting for the sequel of the novel she reads that much." That wasn't really a great comparison but it is on point.

"Avia is a wonderful girl. She will understand but she needs time. You shouldn't stop trying."

Time. At least that is the one thing I have. Mom and I have decided to move back here permanently. My company is opening a photography studio here and I am going to manage that.

However, I wonder how Avia will feel when she hears I have moved back permanently. She will have to see me every day and that will break her heart every single time.

Ughhh, hell. "I'll talk to you later, Mom."

I head to the garage where I had set up a punching bag years ago. I am not the calm kind of guy. And I have a real good temper. Till now I do.

Pushing the hand wraps to the side, I don't need them right now. I use all my energy to punch the bag. Once. Twice. The third time, the bag flies away, torn from the ceiling and slams into the wall. Great.

I think of what Mom said. I should keep trying. I have lost a lot already. No more. I can't let the guilt of what happened in the past destroy my future. Avia is the love of my life and I am not letting her go so easily. She may not forgive me but I don't want her to feel so hurt anymore every time she sees me. I shall fix this.

....

The evening, I head over to the bookstore Avia normally goes to. She comes here every day. I met her for the first time in the coffee shop near the bookstore. Technically, we slammed into each other like we did yesterday.

"Man, do you think this will work?" Jose asks me. My best friend is such a positive guy but he chose right this moment to be negative.

"Can you be a little more optimistic?"

"I am just saying, man."

"It isn't helping."

"Alright. All the best." Jose pats me in the back and heads over to the coffee shop.

I take a deep breath and enter the shop. Avia isn't here. At least I can prepare myself for- the door is pushed open and Avia steps in. She is alone and she doesn't look her cheery self. That is one thing I can take credit for.

I quickly hide myself behind a shelf. I have a plan. I just hope I am not hindered by anything or anyone. God, please help me.

"Do you work here?" some random teenage kid asks me.

"Nope."

"Are you hiding?"

I raise a brow. Who is this kid? And I just prayed for no hindrance. Or did I forget to say 'no'?

"Look, I really have something important to do. So, can you please go ask the shopkeeper your question?"

"He knows why you are hiding here."

Seriously! "Kid," I turn to see Avia at the cash counter. Shit! "Listen, kid. I want you to help me." I hand him over the book I want to give to Avia and point at her. "Just go and give it to the lady there."

"You forgot to say 'please'."

I want to go to hell right now. "Please."

He salutes me then rushes to where Avia is standing and hands her the packet, then motions in my direction. I pretend to be looking somewhere else.

"What is this, Enin?" Avia asks waving the packet in front of my face.

"Hey, angel." Okay, I just blurted that old nickname out. Her face remains blank. "It is your Christmas present. Please, open it."

"What is in it?" that very interesting kid who still hasn't left for some reason questions.

I glare at him. "The shopkeeper is going to give you an extra discount if you disappear from here."

That makes Avia laugh. I stare at her astonished. I just made her laugh. That's one step forward for me. "You haven't changed."

"Not for you. Never for you."

She smiles at me, though the smile doesn't reach her eyes. She opens the wrap and finds the book inside. "Can you keep a secret by Sophie Kinsella?"

"Yup. This was the first movie we watched together at your place because rom-coms were our favourite. Still are, I am hoping."

"Thanks, Enin. But if this-"

I take her hands in mine. "Avia, I know this is a very small gesture. But this is one of the millions I am going to make for you. I am sorry for the way I left you and I can't forgive myself for that. However, I am hoping to at least prove to you that I still love you and I never wanted to leave you."

"I don't know what to say but yeah I still love you too. I just need time."

"Anything for you. Any amount of time you need. I am here forever now."

Avia is about to say something when her phone rings. "It's Dad. Hello, Dad. What? The photographer bailed? I knew he wasn't reliable. Don't worry, I'll find someone else. Bye."

"What happened?" I ask why they are discussing about a photographer when they have me.

"The photographer hired for tomorrow's Christmas party bailed."

"That is not a real problem. You are looking at a pro here."

"So, you want me to give you the project?"

"Hell, yes. If it gives me more time with you."

She smiles, like a real smile and that makes me grin too. "Fine, you got the job, Mr. Ford. Just don't bail on me this time."

"Never."

......

Avia

I can't believe I just agreed to Enin's proposal. I was going to forgive him anyway. He just made it harder not to. Enin has always cared for me and the two years gap hasn't changed that.

Dr. Adyasha Acharya 13

If he and I still love each other, why stay away from each other and hurt ourselves?

It is not worth it.

Dad and Mom are getting dressed up in their room. Grandma is busy choosing champagne glasses for tonight from the cupboard.

The tree has been decorated and will be lit up at midnight, just when Christmas arrives.

There is a knock on the door. "I'll get it," I tell Grandma.

Who has arrived so early? The guests were given a time of 8:00pm. It is two hours early. I open the door to find Enin, dressed in a blue tux, holding a bouquet of roses.

"For you, my angel," he does a dramatic pose and hands me over the bouquet.

"Thank you." I invite him in just at the time my parents come down. They embrace Enin tightly and welcome him exuberantly.

"Your parents still love me like they always did," he nudges me.

"Of course, they do. You are their favourite."

He smirks. "I thought I was yours." I blush. "Hey, we still have time left for the party. Why don't you get dressed and come downstairs real quick? I have a surprise for you." I open my mouth to ask a question but he stops me. "No questions."

"Okay."

I quickly head upstairs to my room and get changed into my beige, pearl-neckline and knee- length dress. I keep my hair down and put on a pair of pearl danglers.

"Mr and Mrs Heming, I am stealing your daughter for an hour. We shall be back before the party."

I just shrug at my parents who laugh. I have no idea what Enin's plan is.

Enin drives me to the main street square by the coffee shop we first met. The whole street is covered with lights and colours.

"What are we doing here?" I question, confused as to what we are doing here on the sidewalk.

"Well, I thought I would tell you how I feel about you at the first place we met."

"You are so creative."

"I know that and I appreciate you noticing it." He takes out his phone and plays a song by Justin Timberlake. "Avia Heming, I want you to know, that you are my best friend, my favourite person, the love of my life and my angel. And I also want to say that I badly want to make you a permanent person in my life so I want you to say that you also love me and that you want me back in your life and that you forgive me."

Tears trickle down my face. "I love you too, Enin."

Enin pulls me closer to him and claims my lips with his. The kiss is soft and tender but it has all his feelings tied to it. "That was the best Christmas gift, I have ever had."

"Me too."

"I am glad I made the decision of coming back here."

"I was missing you badly."

"Now it is my turn to say 'me too'."

Enin and I take a short stroll in the street to enjoy some moments together.

Then we return home in time to welcome the guests. I meet with Enin's mother and give her a tight hug. I had missed her a lot.

Enin clicks the pictures of the guests and in time to time teases me with some random candid clicks of mine.

Honestly, I can't even say anything since his photographs are the best.

Blaire teases me about reconciling with Enin so I return her gratitude by teasing her with Jose. They seem so fond of each other but no one has made the first move yet. I should talk to Enin about it.

"There is just five more minutes to Christmas," I announce for everyone to gather near the tree. It will take everyone atleast five to ten minutes to stop their conversations and come to the living room.

Dad, Mom, Grandma, Enin's mom, Blaire and Jose all gather around along with the other guests. Enin takes his place beside me.

"The countdown, everyone," I clap enthusiastically.

"3…2…1."

Dad lights up the tree with a switch. It is so beautiful. Perfect and bright lights lighting up our house and lives.

"I hope this Christmas brings everyone joy," Mom prays.

"I have another surprise for you," Enin whispers in my ear. He tugs me out of the house to the porch.

"A mistletoe."

"Merry Christmas, Avia."

"Merry Christmas to you too, Enin. You made my Christmas magical."

About the Author

Adyasha Acharya

Dr. Adyasha Acharya is a medical intern in India. She has published novels- The Fearless Warriors, The Guardian and The Defender (The Guardian Series) and many short stories on various national and international magazines.

www.ingramcontent.com/pod-product-compliance
Lightning Source LLC
LaVergne TN
LVHW041603070526
838199LV00047B/2119